...... in Sussex, and spent her early ...... Africa. After working in PR in London, she ....ralia in the 1980s and together with her husband S... ...er own consultancy company, which later evolved into ...ravel publishing house. She is constantly roaming the world ...o research her novels and seeking new storylines, hence the authentic and fascinating detail found in her books.

www.fionamcintosh.com

By Fiona McIntosh

The Lavender Keeper
The French Promise

a&b

The Lavender Keeper

FIONA MCINTOSH

Allison & Busby Limited
12 Fitzroy Mews
London W1T 6DW
www.allisonandbusby.com

First published in Great Britain by Allison & Busby in 2013.
First published by Penguin Group (Australia) 2012.

A CIP catalogue record for this book is available from
the British Library.

First Edition

ISBN 978-0-7490-1344-8

Typeset in 10.5/15.5 pt Sabon by
Allison & Busby Ltd.

The paper used for this Allison & Busby publication
has been produced from trees that have been legally sourced
from well-managed and credibly certified forests.

Printed and bound by
CPI Group (UK) Ltd, Croydon, CR0 4YY

Dedicated to the Crotet family:
Marcel, Françoise, Laurent, Severine and especially
to Louis – a maquisard at sixteen years old –
with whom we shared a meal and friendship
one summer's afternoon in Provence.

PART ONE

CHAPTER ONE

12th July 1942

Luc loved this light on the lavender in summer, just before sunset. The field's hedgerow deepened to glowing emerald and finally to dark sentinels, while the pebbly rows between the mounds of purple blooms became smudges of shadow. The lavender spikes, so straight and tall, never failed to mesmerise him. His gaze was drawn to the bright head of a wild scarlet poppy. No wonder artists flocked to the region in summer, he thought . . . or used to, before the world went mad and exploded with bombs and gunfire.

The young woman next to him did up the top button of her frayed summery blouse. Stray wisps of her long red hair fell across her face to hide grey-green eyes and her irritation. 'You're very quiet,' Catherine said.

Luc blinked out of his reverie, guilty that he'd briefly forgotten she was there. 'I'm just admiring the scenery,' he said softly.

She cut him a rueful glance as she straightened her clothes. 'I wish you did mean me and not your lavender fields.'

He grinned and it seemed to infuriate her. It was obvious Catherine was keen for marriage and children – all the village girls were. Catherine was pretty and much too accommodating, Luc thought, with a stab of contrition. There had been other women in his life, not all so generous, but Catherine obliged because she wanted more. She deserved it – or certainly deserved better. She knew he saw others but she seemed to have a marvellous ability to contain her jealousy, unlike any other woman he'd known.

He brushed some of the tiny purple flowers from her hair and leant sideways to kiss her neck. 'Mmm,' he said. 'You smell of my lavender.'

'I'm surprised I haven't been stung by the bees as well. Perhaps we should consider how nice a bed might be?'

He sensed she was leading up to the question he dreaded. It was time to go. He stood in a fluid motion and offered her a hand. 'I told you, the bees aren't interested in you. Ask Laurent. The bees are greedy for the pollen only.' He waved an arm in a wide arc. 'It's their annual feast and they have a queen to service, young to raise, honey to make.'

She didn't look, busy buckling the belt that cinched her small waist. 'Anyway, Luc, it's not your lavender. It's your father's,' she said. She sounded miffed.

Luc sighed inwardly, wondering whether it was time to tell her the truth. It would be public knowledge soon enough anyway. 'Actually, Catherine, my father has given me all the fields.'

'What?' Her head snapped up, as the expression on her heart-shaped face creased into a frown.

Luc shrugged. He wasn't even sure his sisters knew yet – not that they'd mind – but his annoyance had flared at Catherine's hostile tone. 'On his last trip south he gave them all to me.' He knew he shouldn't enjoy watching her angry eyes dull now with confusion.

'All of them?' she repeated in disbelief.

He opted for a helpless grin. 'His decision, not mine.'

'But that makes you a main landowner for the whole Luberon region. Probably even the largest grower.' It sounded like an accusation.

'I suppose it does,' he replied casually. 'He wants me to take full responsibility for cultivating the lavender. It has to be protected, especially now.' He began to amble away, encouraging her to start the walk home. 'My father spends more time in Paris with his other businesses than he does down here . . . and besides, I was raised in Saignon. He wasn't. This place is in my blood. And the lavender has always been my passion. It's not for him.'

She regarded him hungrily. Now she had even more reason to secure him. But the more she demanded it, the more he resisted. It wasn't that he didn't like Catherine; she was often funny, always sensuous and graceful. But there were aspects of her character he didn't admire, and he disliked her cynicism and lack of empathy. As a teenager he could remember her laughing at one of the village boys who had a stutter, and he knew it was her who'd started a rumour about poor Hélène from the next hamlet. He'd watched, too, her dislocation from the plight of the French under the German regime. For the time being her life was unaffected, and it bothered Luc that her view was blinkered. She never spoke about dreams, only about practicalities – marriage, security, money. Catherine was entirely self-centred.

'I can't think about anything but making these fields as

productive as I can. These aren't times to be planning too far ahead,' he continued, trying to be diplomatic. 'Don't scowl.' He turned to touch her cheek affectionately.

She batted his hand away coldly. 'Luc, Saignon may be in your soul but it doesn't run in your blood.'

When things didn't go Catherine's way she usually struck back. Hers was a cruel barb but an old one. Luc had been an orphan and most of the villagers knew he was an interloper. But he might as well have been born to the Bonet family – he had been only a few weeks old when they took him in, gave him their name and made the tall, pink stone house in the village square his home.

His lighter features set him apart from the rest of his family, and his taller, broader frame singled him out in the Apt region. All he knew was that his ageing language teacher had found him abandoned and had brought him to Saignon, where Golda Bonet, who had recently lost a newborn child of her own, welcomed his tiny body to her bosom, and into her family.

No one knew where he had come from and he certainly didn't care. He loved his father, Jacob, his mother, Golda, and his grandmother, Ida, as well as his trio of dark-haired sisters. Sarah, Rachel and Gitel were petite and attractive like their mother, although Rachel was the prettiest. Luc, with his strong jawline, slightly hooded brow, symmetrical square face and searing blue gaze stood like a golden giant among them.

'Why are you so angry, Catherine?' he asked, trying to deflect this attack.

'Luc, you promised we would be engaged by—'

'I made no such promise.'

He watched her summon every ounce of willpower to control herself; he couldn't help but admire her.

'But you did say we might be married some day.'

'I responded to *your* offer of marriage by saying that "one day we might". That is not an affirmation. You were spoiling for an argument then, as you are now.'

Her large eyes were sparking with anger, and yet again he watched her wrestle that emotion back under control.

'Let's not fight, my love,' she said affectionately, reaching to do up a couple of buttons on his shirt, skimming the skin beneath.

But he did not love Catherine . . . nor want a wife in this chaotic world they found themselves in. If not Catherine, then Sophie or Aurelie in nearby villages, or even gentle Marguerite in Apt would grant him a roll in the hay – or the lavender.

'What are you smiling about?' Catherine asked.

He couldn't tell her he was amused by her manipulative nature. 'Your flushed cheeks. You're always at your prettiest after—'

She put a hand to his lips. 'Please, make an honest woman of me.' She smoothed her skirt. 'We don't even need an engagement; let's just be married and we can make love in a bed as *Monsieur* and *Madame*—'

'Catherine, stop. I have no intention of marrying anyone right now. Let's stop seeing one another if it's causing you so much grief.'

Her expression lost its mistiness; her eyes narrowed and her mouth formed a line of silent anger.

'We are at war,' he reminded her, a plaintive tone in his voice. 'France is occupied by Germans!'

She looked around her, feigning astonishment. 'Where?'

Luc felt a stab of disappointment at her shallow view. Up this high, they were still relatively untroubled by the German soldiers, but his father's letters from Paris were becoming increasingly frantic. The people in the north – in the occupied territories – were suffering enormous economic and social pressure, and those in the capital were bearing the brunt of it.

'So many of those who fled here at the invasion have already gone back north,' Catherine said, sneering. 'All the Parisians have returned. You know it! They're not scared.' She gave a careless shrug. 'It doesn't really affect us. Why should we worry?'

'They've gone back,' he began, quietly despairing, 'because it feels so hopeless. Their homes, their friends, their livelihoods are in the Occupied Zone. They ran south fearing for their lives; they've since decided to learn how to live among the Boches.' He spat on the ground at the mention of the Germans. 'The northerners have no choice. It doesn't mean they like it, or that we have to support the Germans.'

'You'd better not let Gendarme Landry catch you talking like that.'

'I'm not scared of Pierre Landry.'

She looked up at him, shocked. 'Be careful, Luc. He's dangerous.'

'You're the one who should be careful pandering to his demands. I know your family gives him a chicken once a month to stay on his good side.'

Catherine glanced around nervously. 'You're going to get yourself into trouble if you keep talking like that. I don't want to be shot for denouncing the Marshal.'

'Marshal Pétain was a hero in the Great War, but he was not up to the job to lead our nation. Vichy is surely a joke, and now we have the ultimate Nazi puppet leading us. Laval more than dances to Hitler's tune; in fact, he's destroying our great democracy and adopting the totalitarian—'

She covered her ears and looked genuinely anxious. Luc stopped. Catherine was raised as a simple country girl who figured obedience to the Vichy government's militia was the best way for France. And in some respects, perhaps she could be right – but only if you were the sort of person who was content being subservient to a gang of avaricious and racist bullies who were dismantling France's sovereign rights. A *collaborator*! The very word made his gut twist. He didn't know he had such strong political leanings until he'd begun to hear the stories from his father of what it was like to experience Paris – Paris! – being overrun by German soldiers. The realisation that his beloved capital had opened her doors and shrunk back like a cowed dog before Hitler's marauding army had brought disillusionment into his life, as it had for so many young French. It had seemed unthinkable that France would capitulate after all the heroics of the Great War.

His acrimony had hardened to a kernel of hate for the Germans, and on each occasion that German soldiers had ventured close to his home, Luc had taken action.

It was he who thought to blockade the spring, said to date back to Roman times, which fed the famous fountain in the village. By the time the German soldiers, parched and exhausted, had made their way up the steep hill into Saignon, the fountain was no longer running. All the villagers watched the thirsty soldiers drinking from the still water at the fountain's base, smiling as the Germans drank what was reserved for the horses and donkeys of the village. On another occasion he and Laurent had stopped the progress of German motorbikes by felling a tree onto the road. A small win, but Luc was thrilled to see the soldiers, scratching their heads and turning tail.

'One day I'll kill a German for you, Catherine,' Luc promised, unable to fully dampen the fire that had begun to smoulder within.

'I hate it when you talk like this. It frightens me.'

He ran a hand through his hair, realising he was behaving like a bully; she had no political knowledge. After all, if the Luberon kept its collective head down and continued to supply the German war effort with food and produce, this rural part of Provence might escape the war unscathed.

'Listen, I'm sorry that I've upset you,' he began, more gently. 'How about we—' He didn't get any further, interrupted by a familiar voice calling to him.

Laurent appeared, breathless and flushed. He bent over, panting. 'I knew where I'd find you,' he gasped. Laurent glanced shyly at Catherine; he was continually impressed at Luc's way with the local girls.

'What is it?' Luc asked.

'Your parents.'

'What about them?' Immediately Luc's belly flipped. He had a recurring nightmare that his family were all killed – his parents, grandmother, and his three sisters – in some sort of German reprisal for his bad thoughts.

'They're home!' Laurent said excitedly. 'I was sent to find you.'

'Home?' Luc couldn't believe it. 'You mean, Saignon?'

Laurent looked at him as though he were daft. 'Where else do I mean? In the village right now, kissing and hugging everyone. Only you are missing.'

Now Luc's belly flipped for different reasons. He gave Catherine a slightly more lingering kiss than could be considered perfunctory. 'I'll see you soon, eh?'

'When?' she asked.

'Saturday.'

'Today's Saturday!' she snapped.

'Monday, then. I promise.' He reached for her but she slapped his hand away.

She glared at Laurent, who quickly walked a little way off. 'Luc, tell me this. Do you love me?'

'Love? In these uncertain times?'

She gave a sound of despair. 'I've been patient, but if you love me, you will marry me, whether it's now or later. I have to believe in a future. Do you love me?' It came out almost as a snarl.

His long pause was telling. 'No, Catherine, I don't.'

Luc turned and walked away, leaving Catherine stunned, her face hardening into a resolve burning with simmering wrath. 'Your family's money might give you your proud, arrogant air, Luc – but you're just as vulnerable as the rest of us,' she warned.

Laurent's face creased with concern at her words. He cast a despairing look at Luc's back before turning once again to Catherine. 'Will you let me see you home?'

'I'm not helpless, Monsieur Martin,' she said, in a scathing tone.

Laurent's cheeks coloured.

She shrugged. 'As you wish.'

Laurent kept his silence as they made their way back up the hill. He didn't even look around when his shirt got caught on an overhanging branch. He heard it rip, but didn't care about anything right now, other than walking with the woman he had loved since he was a child.

The scene with Catherine was already forgotten; the dash home had cleared Luc's head and by the time he'd made it to the top of the hill, he was feeling relieved that he'd finally spoken plainly to her.

It was young Gitel who saw him first. 'Luc!' she yelled, gleefully running towards him and launching herself into his arms.

He gave a loud grunt. 'What are they feeding you in Paris? Look how tall you've become!' he said, instantly worrying at how petite she seemed. He swung her around, enjoying her squeals of delight. Gitel was nine and Luc loved her exuberance, but she was small for her age and her eyes were sunken. Luc did his best to indulge her, and his elder sisters were always warning him that the way he spoilt Gitel would ruin her perspective on life. He'd scoffed, wondering how any youngster could grow up in Paris since 1939 and not have a skewed view of life. Luc didn't believe any of them could cosset Gitel enough and wished he could persuade his parents to leave her in Saignon. But she was bright and eager to learn at her excellent lycée in Paris. She possessed an ear for music, a sweet voice and a love for the dramatic arts. Her dream was to write a great novel, but while Luc urged her to write down her stories, their father pushed her to keep up her science, her mother insisted on teaching her to sew, and her sisters despaired of her dreamy nature.

'Have you been practising your English?' Luc demanded. 'The world will want to read you in English.'

'Of course,' she replied, in perfect English. 'Have you been keeping up your German?'

It was his father who had insisted he learn German. He urged that the language would be useful in the lavender business in years to come. Luc had not questioned his father's wisdom but had kept his German secret from the villagers.

'Natürlich!' he replied in a murmur. Luc kissed the top of his sister's head. 'Do you think old Wolf is any less relentless?

I suspect your Miss Bonbon allows her junior students to get away with far more.'

Gitel was giggling. 'Bourbon,' she corrected.

He gave her plait a tug and winked.

Gitel's expression changed. 'Papa's not happy. We had to make a mad dash from Paris. He's barely let us pause to sleep and we weren't allowed to stay in any hotels. We slept in the car, Luc! Mama is exhausted.'

Luc caught his father's gaze and immediately saw the tension etched deeply in the set of his mouth, buried beneath a bushy, peppered beard. Jacob Bonet was instructing the housekeeper while amiably continuing a conversation with one of the neighbours. Luc knew him far too well, though, and beneath the jollity he saw the simmering worry in every brisk movement.

A new chill moved through him. Bad news was coming. He could sense it in the air in the same way that he could sense the moment to begin cutting the lavender, whose message also came to him on the wind through its perfume. His beloved saba insisted the lavender spoke to him and him alone. She invested the precious flowers with magical properties, and while her fanciful notions amused Luc, he hadn't the heart to do anything but agree with her.

He watched her now, hobbling out to help with all the possessions that the family had brought south, from his mother's favourite chair to boxes of books. Saba was muttering beneath her breath at all the disruption, but he knew she must be secretly thrilled to have everyone home. It had been just the two of them for a couple of years now.

His grandmother's hands were large for her small, light frame – even tinier now that she was eighty-seven. And those hands had become gnarled and misshapen with arthritis but they were loving, ready to caress her grandson's cheek or waggle an affectionate but warning finger when he teased her. And despite the pain in her joints, she still loved to dance. Sometimes Luc would gently scoop her up like a bird and twirl her around their parlour to music; they both knew she loved it.

'The waltz was the only way a young couple could touch one another, and even through gloves I could feel the heat of your grandfather's touch,' she'd tell Luc, with a wicked glimmer in her eye.

Her hair, once black, was now steely silver, always tied back in a tight bun. He couldn't remember ever seeing her hair down.

He watched the little woman he adored throw her hands apart in silent dismay as Gitel dropped a box.

'Don't worry, Saba. It's only more books!' Luc came up behind the tiny woman and hugged her. 'More hungry mouths to cook for,' he said gently, bending low to kiss. 'Shall I trap some rabbits?'

She reached up to pat his cheek, her eyes filling with happiness. 'We have some chickens to pluck. More than enough. But I might want some fresh lavender,' she whispered and he grinned back. He loved it when Saba flavoured her dishes with his lavender.

'You'll have it,' he promised and planted another kiss on the top of her head.

His elder sisters gave him tight, meaningful hugs. He was shocked at how thin they felt through their summery frocks, and it hurt to watch his mother begin to weep when she saw him. She was all but disappearing – so shrunken and frail.

'My boy, my boy,' she said, as if in lament.

It was all terribly grim for a reunion. 'Why are you crying?' He smiled at his mother. 'We're all safe and together.'

She waved a hand as if too overcome to speak.

'Go inside, my love,' Jacob said in that tender voice he reserved for his wife. 'We can manage this. Girls, help your mother inside. I need to speak with your brother.'

'Let me—' Luc began, but his father stilled him with a hand on his arm.

'Come. Walk with me.' Luc had never heard his normally jovial father as solemn.

'Where are you going?' Sarah complained softly. 'We've only just arrived.'

Luc smiled at his eldest sister, trying his best to ignore the way her shoulders seemed to curve inwards, adding to her hollow look. 'I'll be back in a heartbeat,' Luc whispered to her. 'I want to know everything about Paris.'

'Be careful what you wish for,' Sarah warned, and the sorrow in her tone pinched Luc's heart.

CHAPTER TWO

Luc fell in step with his father, who now appeared brittle enough to snap. 'It's so good to have you all back, but if we'd known, we could have made arrangements.' He laid a hand across the older man's shoulders and not even his father's clothes could conceal the blades, hard and angular, that jutted beneath.

'No time,' Jacob admitted brusquely. 'Where's Wolf? I sent him a message ahead.'

'We were planning a meal together tonight anyway. Saba is cooking his favourite.'

'Good. I need to talk with him.' His father sighed and looked up. 'I used to run up this hill.'

Luc had registered his father's far slower tread. 'Are you well, Papa?'

His father looked down and Luc was astonished to see his lip quiver. 'I don't know what I am, son. But I am glad to see you.' He linked arms with Luc. 'Now, help me up this wretched hill. I would see my favourite valley from our lookout.'